HANK THE COWDOG.

THE CASE OF THE SWIRLING KILLER TORNADO

John R. Erickson

Illustrations by Gerald L. Holmes

Maverick Books
Published by Gulf Publishing Company
Houston, Texas

P9-AQI-552

For Trev Tevis,
whose heroic struggle against pain
has not diminished the beauty of his music.

Maverick Books
Published by Gulf Publishing Company
P. O. Box 2608, Houston, Texas 77252-2608

10   9   8   7   6   5   4   3

Library of Congress Cataloging-in-Publication Data

Erickson, John R., 1943–
     Hank the Cowdog : the case of the swirling killer tornado / John R. Erickson ; illustrations by Gerald L. Holmes.
         p.   cm.   — (Hank the Cowdog ; 25)
     Summary: Hank the cowdog and his sidekick Drover find themselves confronting a huge storm in the middle of the night.
     ISBN 0-87719-279-0 (hardcover). — ISBN 0-87719-278-2 (pbk.). — ISBN 0-87719-280-4 (cassette)
     1. Dogs—West (U.S.)—Fiction.   2. Ranch life—West (U.S.)—Fiction.
[1. Dogs—Fiction.   2. West (U.S.)—Fiction.   3. Tornadoes—Fiction.
4. Humorous stories.]   I. Title.   II. Series: Erickson, John R., 1943–
Hank the Cowdog ; 25.
PS3555.R428H34   1995
813'.54—dc20   95-21672
                                                                          CIP
                                                                          AC

Printed in the United States of America.

C O N T E N T S

Have you read all of Hank's adventures?
Available in paperback at $6.95:

Also available on cassettes:
Hank the Cowdog's Greatest Hits!

CHAPTER

1

A TEMPEST IN A TEABAG

It's me again, Hank the Cowdog. It was June, as I recall, the middle of June. I was under the gas tanks, sleeping on my gunnysack bed.

Or resting my eyes, would be closer to the truth. See, it was almost midnight and I am never asleep at that hour. Never. The Head of Ranch Security is always wide awake, alert, and on night patrol during the deep dark hours of the night.

I was resting mine eyes. Drover, on the other hand, was totally knocked out: snoring, grunting, wheezing, jerking, twitching, fluttering his eyelids, squeaking, and doing all the other things he does in his sleep.

He was starting to get on my nerves. I cracked one eyelid and addressed him in a firm term of voice: "Droving, must you snork all that guttersnipe? Plumber's friend porkchop and horrifying bananas."

"Snork murk rumple wrinkle skittle rickie tattoo."

I couldn't help chuckling at that. I mean, to who or whom did he think he was speaking? "Whittle wheelbarrowing fodder-fiddle's whickerbill."

"Mugg wump tree trunk. Norking smurk whiffle feathers on Tuesday."

"I donkey that. Horse hoof jellybean bonk woofer clock spring."

"Rubbard pillowfight?"

"Omelet."

"Yeah, but cornbread highway."

"Tell your spaghetti leaves to double-clutch the peanut butter."

"Beanstalk bird nest horizontal chickenpox."

All at once it occurred to me that this conversation was going nowhere. Drover was making very little sense and I was a busy dog. I didn't have time to listen to his foolishness.

I cracked my other eyelid and beamed him a look of purest steel. "Drover, if you're going to talk to me, the least you can do is snork mirk the posthole diggers."

His head came up. His eyes drifted open and moved around in little circles. "Who ate the trees?"

2

"I can't answer that. The point is . . ." I blinked my eyes several times and slowly Drover's face came into focus. Perhaps I had been asleeper than I thought. "The point is that I don't know what you're talking about."

"Oh. Then what about the spare tire?"

"I still don't know what you're talking about."

He gave his head a shake, stood up, and walked around in a circle. "Gosh, I don't know what I've been talking about either."

"There, you see? Exactly my point. You've been talking nonsense, which makes me think, Drover, that you've been asleep. Is it possible that you're still asleep, even though we're in the most dangerous part of the night?"

"Well, I . . . I'm not sure. What is today?"

"Today is today, Drover, the very day in which we are living and breathing.

"Oh. Well, if it's already today, there's no need for us to wait around for it. We might as well take a little nap."

I thought about that for a moment. "Good point. A little nap sometimes does wonders."

"Yeah, and it'll help us wake up later on."

"Exactly. Studies show that dogs who take naps are more likely to snork and murgle than scrambled tumbleweeds."

My eyes drifted shut. My breathing fell into a deep and regular pattern. It was very quiet and peaceful. Then . . .

"Hank, are you sleepy?"

"Huh?"

"I said, are you sleepy?"

"No thanks, I couldn't hold another bite."

"'Cause I'm not. All at once I'm wide awake. Did you hear that sound?"

"Chinese tunafish."

"I heard it. I heard it with my own ears. Hank, are you asleep?"

"Saddle blanket salad poofly murgle porkchop."

"Hank, you'd better wake up. I just heard a sound and I'm getting scared and my leg hurts."

I opened my head and lifted my eyes . . . lifted my head and opened my eyes, I should say, and tried to bring Drover's folks into the fracas . . . Drover's face into focus, actually.

Perhaps I had dozed, but not deeply and not for long. I tried to bring Drover's face into focus. "Did you just say that your leg heard a sound?"

"No, I said that my leg hurts but my ears heard a sound."

"Okay, that checks out. There for a minute, I thought . . . where are we, Drover?"

"Well, I think we're under the gas tanks, and I think you woke up for a minute and fell asleep again."

"Ha, ha. I don't think so. No, I was just planning out the day's agenda."

"Yeah, but it's the middle of the night."

"Exactly. That's what I mean. No problem." I pushed myself up on all fours and shook the vapors out of my head. "Where did you say we were?"

"When?"

"Right now, you tuna."

"Well, under the gas tanks . . . I guess."

"Yes, of course. Good. We're right on schedule. I had scheduled a meeting here under the, uh, gas tanks. Do you know the purpose of this meeting?"

"Well, let's see." He rolled his eyes. "You wanted to hear my new song?"

"What?"

"I wrote a song. In my sleep. While I was asleep, I thought of this song, just kind of dreamed it up out of nowhere."

I stared at the runt. "You wrote a song in your sleep? That sounds crazy, Drover. In the first place, you don't even sing. I mean, dogs who don't sing don't write songs."

"Yeah, I know, but I did, I really did. It came to me in a dream. It's about tornadoes."

"Oh brother. In the middle of the night, you're composing a song about tornadoes?"

"Yeah, you want to hear it? I'd better do it pretty quick or I'll forget it."

"And that would be a tragedy, I suppose."

"Yeah, 'cause I never wrote a song before."

"You already said that."

"I'm kind of proud of it."

"Yes, of course." I yawned. "Okay, let's hear it. Might as well get it over with."

"Oh good! But I don't know what key it's in."

"Just sing the song, Drover, and let's get on to something else."

"Okay. Here I go."

In case you're interested, here's the song.

Drover's Tornado Safety Song

Never ever bark at a funnel-shaped
    cloud
If it's spinning in a circle and
    roaring real loud.
See, it could be a monster or a
    goblin or a spook
Or something else entirely worse
    that mightn't turn you loose.

Turn me loose, turn me loose, I'm
    as silly as a goose
For barking at a thing that's bigger
    than a moose.
If you bark up a storm, then one
    might appear,
You'll get an education, and
    knocked on your rear.

On your rear, on your rear, on your
    hiniest rear,
It'll knock you on your can and
    stand you on your ear.
Spin you in a circle and circle all
    around,
You'll fly through the air and skid
    across the ground.

Cross the ground, cross the
    ground, cross the cold hard
    ground,
You'll lose a lot of sleep and hair
    by the pound.
There's quite a bit of difference
    'tween a storm and a frog.
A storm doesn't have much fear of
    a dog.

Here's the moral to the story of the
    funnel-shaped cloud
That's spinning in a circle and
    roaring real loud.
If you bite a big tornado it'll
    probably give you hiccups
So take this piece of good advice:
    go back to barkin' pickups.

He finished the song and sat there, grinning and waiting for me to say something. "What do you think? Tell me the truth."

"What do I think? Well . . . it's a song, Drover, we can't deny that. I mean, it has words and sort of a melody."

"Yeah, but do you like it? I thought it had a pretty deep message: stay away from tornadoes. I guess you could say that it promotes tornado safety."

I rose from my gunnysack bed and took a big stretch. It appeared that my rest time was over. I began pacing in front of Young Beethoven. My mind works better when I pace, don't you see.

"Okay, Drover, you asked for my opinion and I'll give it. Number One, the song wasn't as silly as I had expected. But, Number Two, it was silly enough. Because, Number Three, we have never had a tornado on this ranch. Hence, Number Four, what you have created—if you actually wrote it— what you have there is a tempest in a teabag."

He gave me his patented blank stare. "What does that mean?"

"It means, Drover, that you've written a song without a deep underlying purpose." Suddenly I stopped pacing and whirled around to face him. "If we don't have tornadoes, Drover, we don't need a song that promotes tornado safety."

"Gee, I never thought of that."

I gave the little mutt a pat on the back. "But you tried, Drover, that's the important thing. There's an old saying that fits this situation: 'Better to try and do something really stupid than not to try at all.'"

"There's that sound again."

"I beg your pardon?"

"I heard a sound, kind of like . . . thunder, distant thunder."

I lifted my eyes to the sky above and studied the weather patterns and so forth. "Drover, I see stars."

"Yeah, but . . . "

"Let me finish. Stars twinkle but they have never been known to produce thunder."

"Yeah but . . . "

"Hence, it follows from simple logic that . . . " KA-BOOM! " . . . yikes, that we're being attacked by an enormous thunderstorm . . . holy smokes, look at the lightning in that cloud!"

"Yeah, and I'm scared of storms!"

"Battle Stations, Drover, and prepare to defend the ranch!"

"Oh, my leg!"

And with that, we went streaking up the caliche hill behind the house and prepared to do battle

with one of the most dangerous enormous storms
I'd encountered in my whole career.

And what made it even worse was that I hadn't
slept a wink in days. No kidding.

CHAPTER

2

THE SCRAMBLED EGG MYSTERY

Did I say that *we* went streaking up the hill?

I went streaking up the hill. I ran. I threw my entire heart and soul into the effort. Drover, on the other hand, limped and lollygagged, cried and complained every step of the way.

But we did manage to establish a position near the yard gate. There, I halted the column and prepared our defense of the ranch.

Most of the time, our spring storms track from the southwest to the northeast, and they usually occur in the late afternoon. In other words, a guy can see them building up and can prepare for them.

This one was different. It was one of those sneaky storms that build up after dark and come rolling in after everyone has gone to bed.

The first sign of trouble is the twinkle of distant lightning in the distance. Then the wind will rise, and most generally it's a moist wind. Then a guy will begin to hear grumbles of thunder, and by that time, fellers, you'd better be in Battle Stations.

We were. We'd made it just in time. I marched back and forth in front of the troops.

"All right, men, we've seen the enemy. At first glance, he appears to be huge and awesome, but I want to remind you that he puts on his pants just the way we do. Any questions?"

Drover raised his paw. "If we don't wear pants, can we go hide in the machine shed?"

"No. The pants business was just a figure of speech, Drover, and I'd be grateful if you'd try to be more serious."

"I am serious. I'm seriously scared of storms."

"Yes, and that's one of your problems. You're too serious about everything. You have no sense of humor. Any more questions?" Drover raised his paw. "Yes? You in the back."

"What should we do with the wounded?"

I continued pacing. "The wounded. Good question. I hadn't actually worked through that one, but yes, we need to have a contagency plan for the wounded. Hmmm. Okay, here we go. We'll have to establish a field hospital in the machine shed and try to get the wounded in there as soon as possible."

"Got it. See you around."

If I hadn't stopped the little mutt, he would have gone streaking to the machine shed. "Hold it, stop right there, halt. You're not excused, and where do you think you're going?"

"Well, I was fixing to rush me to the hospital."

"We haven't even barked a shot yet."

"Yeah, but this old leg is just tearing me up."

"Soldier, I'm fixing to tear up another part of your anatomy if you don't hold your position. We're in Battle Stations and the enemy is approaching. Get back to your post, and that's a direct order."

"Oh darn."

"And I will not tolerate cursing and swearing in this outfit."

"Oh drat."

"There you go again. For cursing and swearing in the line of duty, you get three Shame-On-You's."

"Oh phooey."

"Make that six, Drover. You want to go for nine?"

"Sure, might as well."

"Okay, pal, you want to buck the system and be a little rebel, so you're up to nine Shame-On-You's."

"Oh fiddle."

"There's twelve. How about fifteen? You want to shoot for bigger numbers, huh? We've got time. Go ahead, get it out of your system."

"I thought I was bucking the system."

"You're bucking against life, Drover."

"I knew a bucking horse one time."

"Yes, and what did it get him? He bucked and he bucked and he bucked, and what did it get him? Tell me."

"Well, he pitched Slim through the saddle shed door."

"Exactly. And do you see what all this means?"

"Not really."

"It means . . . it means that you have twelve Shame-On-You's on your record. Do you want to go for fifteen?"

"No, I'm out of naughty words."

"Good. Twelve's bad enough. If you ever try to get another ranch job, those Shame-On-You's will be on your record. Everyone will know what a rotten little mutt you really are, and do you think anybody will offer you a job?"

"I wouldn't."

"Neither would I, Drover. In fact, with your lousy record, I'm not sure you have a place in our Security Division. How does that make you feel?"

"Can I go to the machine shed?"

"No."

"Shucks."

"There's eighteen, Drover. You keep piling them up."

"I think it's only fifteen."

"Fifteen, eighteen, what's the difference?"

"Columbus discovered America in 1518."

"Yes, and the reason he discovered America was that he didn't stand around cursing and swearing. He sailed his ships. He studied the stars. He wrote in his log."

"Slim burns logs in his stove."

"That's exactly my point, Drover. Do you want to burn logs or sail across the ocean?"

"Well . . . I don't like water."

"Exactly. And if you continue this pattern of foul language, you'll spend your whole life . . . hmmm, was that a raindrop?"

"I think it was the ocean."

"What?"

"Columbus sailed across the ocean, but at the end of every ocean there's a pot of raindrops."

I walked several steps away and gazed off at the approaching storm. I took a deep breath and let the wind blow my ears around.

"Drover, I must tell you something."

"Sure, anything."

"Sometimes I think the stress of this job is too much for me. I . . . I'll be honest. Now and then I feel that . . . that the things I'm saying . . . just don't make sense."

"I'll be derned."

"Please don't curse and swear."

"Sorry. I won't be derned. I'll never be derned."

"Thanks. I hope you mean that."

"Oh, I do."

"Good. Drover, sometimes . . . sometimes I have this, this strange sensation that . . . my mind is a bowl of scrambled eggs. Have you ever had that feeling?"

"Boy, I love eggs."

"I know, but I'm talking about the sensation of scrambled eggs. Have you ever felt that your entire life, all your thought processes, your plans and dreams . . . were coming out of a bowl of scrambled eggs?"

"Well, let's see. Nope, never have."

"Hmmm. Just as I thought. It's this job, the crushing responsibility, the ozone we breathe day after day at the top of the mountain."

I heaved a deep sigh, walked back to Drover, and laid a paw on his shoulder.

"I'm glad we've had this opportunity to chat. It's so seldom that I get to, well, chat with the men."

"Yeah, or even with us dogs."

"Exactly." I gazed up at the stars which were now covered with thick clouds and were therefore invisible. "The hour is late, Drover, and the night is dark. What are we doing here by the yard gate?"

"Well, let's see. I don't remember. Do you reckon we're waiting for scraps?"

"Maybe so, although I don't remember Sally May ever bringing out scraps in the middle of the night."

"Yeah, and if she's not going to bring out scraps, it doesn't make much sense for us to be waiting for them. I guess."

"Good point, son. Maybe we should go back to bed."

"Boy, I can go for that."

"I don't know about you, but I'm worn to a frazzle, completely bushed. This patrol work is a dog-killer. We've earned a rest."

And with that, we made our respective ways down the caliche hill and to our gunnysack beds beneath the gas tanks. We had hardly seen those beds in the past forty-eight hours.

I fluffed up my gunnysack, walked around it three times, and collapsed. The bone-deep fatigue that had gripped me moments before seemed to rise like a helium balloon and float out through a window in the top of my snork, murking the porkchop snicklefritz.

Zzzzzzzzzzzzzzzzzzzzzzzzzzzzzzzzzzzzzzzzzzzzzzzz.

C H A P T E R

3

HEADQUARTERS IS ATTACKED BY CHARLIE MONSTERS

The mortar and cannon fire began shortly after one o'clock. Two o'clock. We had no clock so we weren't sure when the enemy began his merciless artillery barrage.

Suddenly shells were falling all around us—mortars, bazookas, 83's, 44's. Charlie was throwing everything he had into this bombardment.

I heard the artillery shells falling in the distance but my sleeping mind tried to ignore them. I mean, my poor body was SO exhausted from overwork and lack of sleep and so forth, SO EXHAUSTED that it cried out and begged for just one more minute of precious sleep.

But as the shelling moved closer to our command post, I found it impossible and impossibler to ignore the obvious: that Headquarters had come under a withering attack. And when a shell from one of Charlie's big 88's ripped through a tree nearby, I was forced to leave the scented vapors of sleep and rally the troops for battle.

KA-BOOOM!

G.L. Holmes

But just a word here about my use of technical military terms, such as "Charlie's big 88's." I realize that most people and dogs aren't accustomed to using such heavy-duty terms, which is fine because most people and dogs don't have a need for such a complex and ultra-secret method of communication.

The fact that we do—WE meaning those of us who are involved every day in security work—the fact that we use these extremely complicated and secret words doesn't necessarily mean that the rest of you are . . . how can I say this?

It doesn't necessarily mean that you're too dumb to understand, although . . . you're just busy with other things, that's all, so let's go to the blackboard and learn some of these special words and terms.

First off, we have the word "Charlie." Charlie is a common name, often used for people, horses, and even a few dogs. But when WE in the Security Business use the word, it means—pay close attention to this next part—it means The Enemy.

Exactly who is this enemy? We're never sure. All we can say for sure is that the Charlies are the guys behind those big 88's.

And that brings us to the next major term in our list of major terms. "88" is actually a shortened version of the longer version of the name of what it is, and what it is is a huge enormous gun.

A cannon. A huge cannon so big and awesome that the south end isn't even connected to the north end. Well, that might be a slight exaggeration. I mean, it's hard to imagine something so huge that the two ends . . .

It's big, that's the point, real big, and it shoots an arterial shell that is also very large, and we're talking about something as big as, oh, a trash barrel. Or maybe as big as a pickup. Or a whole house.

In other words, really really big and huge and enormous, and that's why those shells make such a loud noise when they come crashing down to earth.

Perhaps you think I've forgotten the most important part of this heavy-duty discussion of technical terms—what the number "88" means. No, I didn't forget, not at all. I was saving it for last because, well, I get a kick out of tossing out those names and numbers which mean nothing to everybody else.

It gives me a thrill.

Okay, let's go public with it. There are several ways of looking at "88," and the interesting thing is that it looks pretty muchly the same whether you look at it right-side-up or wrong-side-down.

You don't believe me? Try it. See, I told you.

Another way of approaching this mystery is that if you add the two numbers together, that is,

8 + 8, you get 17. No, scratch that. You get 16. 8 + 8 = 16. That sounds better. You get 16, and do you know what that means?

It means nothing. Charlie does this to confuse us, don't you see. He knows that our intelligence officers are working day and night to break his codes, and so he does things to foul up our systems.

They're very clever. Never underestimate the cunning of the Charlies.

They never sleep, those guys, but neither do we.

It's a constant game of cat and mouse.

Where was I? Oh yes, the mysterious double meaning of "88." We have shown that "88" has no double meaning, that it's just another of Charlie's tricks, which leaves us with just one stern untoned.

Stone unturned.

If "88" has no double meaning, does it have a single meaning? Good question, and the answer is yes. The complete technical term for this huge artillery piece is "Oldsmobile 88." In the heat of battle, we shorten that to "88," and there you are.

It takes a lot of time to explain all this stuff but we think it's pretty derned important.

Anyways, the barrage had begun and the 88's were falling like rain all around our bunker, and you never heard such a deafening roar. Perhaps I had drifted off into a light, uh, slumbering mode, not really sleep, and when the first 88 landed nearby, I leaped to my feet and sounded the alarm.

Actually, I ran into the angle iron leg of the gas tanks and did some pretty serious damage to the old nose, but then I began shouting the alarm.

"Drover, Battle Stations! Red Alert! They're coming, they're on the outskirts of the city! Headquarters is being overrun by thousands and thousands of little green Charlies!"

Drover flew out of his gunnysack and began running in circles—squeaking. "Oh my gosh, help, murder, monsters, where's my leg!"

Just then, there was a blinding flash of light and a window-rattling explosion. And Drover went down.

I rushed to his side. "Drover, speak to me. I think you've been hit."

"I can't speak, I've been hit!"

"That's okay. Save your strength. Don't try to talk. Where does it hurt?"

"Well, let's see. Here and here and here, and there too."

"Sounds pretty bad, son, but of course I can't see all those wounds because it's very dark. Can you be more specific?"

"I'll try, Hank, I'll give it my best shot, but the pain's terrible."

"I understand but don't try to talk. Just tell me where the pain is located."

"Which one?"

"I don't know, Drover, just pick a pain and tell me where it's located."

"Well, it seems to be coming from . . . "

"Yes, yes?"

"The pain, the terrible pain seems to be . . . in my leg."

"Uh oh. That's the very worst kind."

"Yeah, and maybe we'd better rush me up to the machine shed."

"Hmmm. You could be right. Can you make it on your own or do I need to carry you?"

Another incoming shell lit up the night and shook the earth. KA-BOOOOOOM!

Drover squeaked. "Well, I can try to make it, but I may have to limp."

"That's okay, soldier. Out here on the front lines, nobody would dare laugh at you because you have a limp."

He limped around in a circle and . . . for some reason, it struck me as funny and I found myself . . . laughing, you might say. I know. It was crazy, but I couldn't help it.

He gave me a hurtful look. "Are you laughing at me?"

"What? Laughing at . . . don't be absurd, Drover. I've already ha ha told you that hee hee nobody would dare ho ho . . . "

KA-BLOOOOEY! KA-BOOM! KA-BAM!

The roar of incoming artillery pretty muchly took care of the funny business, and to make matters even worse, the wind was rising and rain was coming down in sheets and buckets.

What lousy luck, to get a rainstorm right on top of an Enemy attack. All at once this was no laughing matter, no matter how ridiculous Drover looked limping around, and the time had come for us to run for our lives.

"Drover, we've got to make a run for it. They've stormed headquarters and now it's every dog for himself!"

"Oh my gosh, which way's the machine shed?"

"Forget the machine shed. We'd better retreat to the house and sound the alarm. Come on, son, to the yard gate!"

"Oh my gosh, what about my limp?"

"Bring it along. You might need it."

And with that, our sad little column abandoned Command Post One and staggered up the hill, against wind and pouring rain and incredible odds. No ordinary dog could have led his troops up that hill, but somehow I managed to do it.

We halted at the yard gate. Shells were exploding all around us. The yard gate was shut.

"Drover," I yelled over the wind and rain, "this gate is shut. Can you jump the fence?"

"I don't think so, Hank. This old leg is just barely hanging on."

"Okay, here's the plan. I'll jump the fence and make a dash for the porch. You hold this position as long as you can, and if you get captured by the Charlie Monsters . . . "

"You know, it's feeling a little better now. I'll give it a try."

"Okay, trooper. See you at the porch, and good luck."

I coiled my legs under me and went flying over the fence, landed on the other side, and sprinted across the yard to the safety of the porch. And I'll be derned, Drover was already there—dripping rainwater and shivering.

"Nice work, son, but we don't have a minute to spare. We've got to sound the alarm and warn Sally May and Loper. I'll bark and you moan. Ready? Let 'er rip!"

And with that, we threw ourselves into the very dangerous task of moaning, barking, and warning our friends that the Charlie Monsters had invaded our ranch.

C H A·P T E R

4

THE POLKA-DOT MIDGET

As you might have already guessed already, initiating the Moan and Bark Maneuver revealed our location to all the Charlies.

See, by that time the Charlie Monsters had advanced and captured most of the important positions around Headquarters, and even though we couldn't exactly see them, we knew they were there.

Yes, we knew they were there, sprinting from building to building on their hairy green legs and setting up listening devices that would zero in on the sounds of our barking. It was just a matter of time until they found us, and then . . . gulp.

We didn't have a moment to spare. Huddled together on the back porch, pressing our dripping bodies against the screen door, we barked and moaned. And then we moaned and barked. We HAD to get word of the attack to Loper and Sally May, because if we failed in this mission . . . gulp again.

But our best barking and moaning had no effect. No lights came on in the house. No one opened the door to let us in. No one rushed outside to help us defend our position.

Things were looking pretty bad.

KA-BLOOEY!

Another 88 exploded nearby, and in that brief but brilliant flash of light I saw . . .

"Drover, did you see what I just saw?"

"I don't think so. I've got my eyes covered with my paws. What was it?"

"I'm almost sure I saw . . . a bunch of little green Monster Men."

"Oh my gosh!"

"Each one of 'em had six legs, Drover, six hairy green legs. And big heads with three eyes. They're out there running around in the rain and mud."

"Oh my gosh, they're looking for US!"

"I'm afraid you're right."

"And if we keep on barking, they'll find us."

"Exactly."

"Oh Hank, I want to go home!"

"You are home, Drover, but I don't think this is what you had in mind."

"It's not. Do you reckon they eat dogs?"

"Oh sure, no question about it. They eat dogs until they're full and then they eat some more, just for sport."

I could feel the little mutt shivering. "What are we going to do?"

"I was just asking myself that same question, Drover. We've failed to wake up Loper and Sally May with our barking. The only course of action left to us is to . . . chew our way into the house."

I heard him gasp. "Chew our way . . . you mean, through the door?"

"Exactly. We'll take out the screen door first and then go to work on the wooden door."

"Gosh, won't they be mad?"

"Sure, they'll be mad. They'll be furious. After all, they want to eat us."

"Oh my gosh! You mean Loper and Sally May want to eat us too?"

"What?"

"Even our friends want to eat us!"

"Wait a minute. I'm talking about the Charlie Monsters. Who or whom are you talking about?"

"Well . . . I thought maybe Loper and Sally May would be mad if we chewed up their doors."

"Oh. No, quite the contrary, Drover. If they were here right now, I'm sure they'd want us to chew down the doors, the walls, or whatever to save ourselves. Do you think they'd want to lose their entire Security Division?"

"Well, I hope not."

"Believe me, son, they'll be delighted to see us. Now, let's go to work on this screen. Go to Full Claws and Teeth."

Boy, you should have seen us digging on that screen door! We hit it with Full Claws and Teeth, and in just a matter of a few minutes, we had taken it out. You'd have thought we had chainsaws for teeth.

I paused for a moment to catch my breath and to admire our work. And spit splinters.

"Nice work, son. That screen didn't have much of a chance against us, did it? Ha! They thought they had us trapped! Little did they know."

"Yeah, but that was the easy part. The next door won't be so easy."

"Stand back and watch this. Hank the Cowdog is fixing to show you how we take out a wooden door." I loosed up the muscles in my enormous shoulders and also the powerful muscles in my jaws. "In two minutes, we'll be inside the house. Watch."

I threw my entire body and soul into the task of mowing down that door. I had become a chainsaw,

G.L. Holmes

a battering ram, a sludgehammer, a powerful laser-driven machine that was totally dedicated to the task of . . .

Some doors are thicker than you might suppose. This one proved to be pretty stubborn. I mean, chips and sawdust were flying everywhere, and my teeth were throwing up sparks and my claws were ripping huge hunks of wood from . . .

I stopped to rest. Drover was watching. "How's it going?"

"Piece of cake. We're almost there. Just a few more bites and we'll be inside the house."

I took a gulp of air and hit it again, this time with the fury of . . . nobody had warned me that this particular door was ten inches thick and made of solid oak.

I mean, we're talking about a door that must have weighed, oh, five hundred pounds. It's a wonder they could find hinges to hold it up, and I doubt that any dog in the world could have . . .

And did I mention that it was covered with steel armored plate? Yes sir, one inch of solid steel, bolted into ten inches of solid oak, and I soon realized that if I kept up my frenzy of chewing, I would soon be toothless.

I stopped to catch my breath and spit wood. Steel, that is, from the steel plate.

Again, Drover was watching. "How's it going now?"

I gave him a withering glare and was about to give him worse than that when, all of a sudden and before our very eyes, the door opened.

I turned a worldly smile upon my companion. "As you can see, Drover, the door gave up."

"You mean, it opened itself?"

"Of course it did. That door knew that if it didn't yield to my powerful attack, it would soon be nothing but splinters and sawdust. You probably thought . . . "

HUH?

Yikes, someone was standing in the gloomy darkness in front of us. A small person, perhaps a midget, dressed in a strange red and white polka-dot uniform.

I felt the hair rising on the back of my neck and a deep ferocious growl began to rumble in my . . .

Okay, relax. Did you think it was one of the green Charlie Monsters? Ha, ha, ha. No, not at all.

Little Alfred. Wearing red and white polka-dot pajamas. Ha, ha, ha. See, I had known, or had suspected . . .

Never mind.

It was our friend, Little Alfred, not a Charlie Monster, and that was the best news of the year. I almost fainted with relief. Or to view it at a slightly different angle, *Drover* almost fainted with relief, while I was merely glad to see him.

Little Alfred, that is. I was glad to see Little Alfred, not Drover. I had been with him all night and that was one night too many.

The boy switched on the utility room light and stared at the, uh, screen door, the damaged screen door. His eyes grew wide and his mouth fell open.

"Ummmmmmm!"

At that very moment, I decided the time had come to switch all circuits over to Innocent Looks and Slow Tail Thumping. I mean, "Ummmmmm" is sort of a tip-off word, right? It warns of stormy weather ahead, so to speak.

"You dogs wecked the scween door and my mom's gonna be MAD!"

I found myself fidgeting and turning my gaze away from the, uh, screen door, and generally feeling uncomfortable about the whole thing. The very mention of Alfred's mom brought back a rush of unpleasant memories—our many misunderstandings, a relationship that had known its share of ups and downs, being chased around the yard by an angry ranch wife and her broom.

"Hankie, how come you wecked the scween?"

Well, I . . . that is, we thought . . . there were all these huge loud explosions and . . . well, Charlie Monsters running around all over the place and . . .

"Were you doggies scared of the storm?"

Storm? Oh no. Storms had never bothered me. What had scared me and Drover . . . well, mainly

Drover, what had scared Drover had been something much bigger and far more serious than your average little . . .

"Well," the boy dropped his voice to a whisper, "it scared me too, all that thundoo and wightning."

Oh?

The boy was scared, huh? Well, yes, storms were, uh, pretty scary things. The big ones, that is, your major summer thunderstorms, we're talking about. Pretty scary.

"Do you doggies want to come into the house so we can be scared together?"

Come into the . . . no, we had Night Patrol and many other . . . there really wasn't time in our busy . . .

But when he opened what was left of the screen door, I suddenly realized that taking care of the kids and making sure they got a good night's sleep was the very most important job for every ranch dog and . . .

Okay, what the heck, we had time. If it would make Sally May's child sleep better and feel more secure . . .

KA-BOOOM!

We flew into the house . . . which might not have been one of the smartest things we ever did.

CHAPTER

5

THE BACON TEMPTATION

I went straight to the rug which lay in the middle of the utility room floor. There, I laid down and ordered Drover to do the same.

I wanted Little Alfred to know, and to SEE through our very actions, that our motives here were as pure as the driveled snow, and that we had every intention of being good dogs in the house.

I mean, some of your lower-class dogs will take advantage of every situation and every little gesture of kindness. You let 'em into the house and they go nuts.

Not us, fellers. We knew our place: on that rug in the utility room. That's all we needed or wanted, just a warm dry place in the same area of the house where the cowboys took off their dirty boots and spurs. That was plenty good for us.

Shucks, we didn't need to go even one step farther into Sally May's clean house. A ranch dog had no business in the kitchen or the living room anyways.

The utility room was just fine, and we laid down on that rug and became models of Perfect Dog Behavior in the House.

Alfred looked at us. "Are you gonna sweep out here?"

Oh yeah, sure, fine. Perfect place to sleep. We were just glad to have a dry rug and a roof over our heads.

He wrinkled his nose. "Pew! You doggies are wet and you stink."

Yes, well, the Wet Dog Smell wasn't one of my favorites either, but sometimes a guy can't help how he smells. We were doing the best we could.

I mean, we don't try to stink. We don't wake up in the morning and say, "Gosh, I think I'll stink today." Those things just happen.

"Well, nighty night." He turned out the light and went back to bed.

Ah yes, this was the life! No dog could have asked for more. Outside in the Cruel World, the lightning tore through the dark fabric of night and the thunder boomed and the rain made a steady roar on the . . .

It was a thunderstorm, see. Perhaps you had

G.L. Holmes

thought it was an invasion of Charlie Monsters and, okay, there for a few minutes I had thought so too, but the evidence was beginning to point toward a thunderstorm instead of an invasion.

At first glance, they are very similar. Every dog gets fooled once in a while, and it's no disgrace, no big deal.

I stretched out on the rug and surrendered my grip on the world. At last, no cares or responsibilities, just a warm, dry porkchop to snorking mork sniffer, but there was a light shining in my eyes.

"Drover, turn out the light, will you?"

"Rumple snuffbox chicken feather."

"Drover, I said . . . "

I sat up and cracked open one eye and . . . a light? A beam of light, cutting through the darkness and stabbing me in the retinas? I was about to deliver a Warning Bark to the whoever-it-was when, much to my surprise, I heard a whispering voice, which I recognized as Little Alfred's.

It appeared that he had crept back out to the utility room and was now wielding a lighted flashlight.

"Doggies, I'm scared. Want to come sweep in my woom?"

Come into his room? I ran that one through my data banks and received a confirmation of my first reaction: That wasn't a great idea.

Why, the very thought of moving deeper into a house which contained a potentially deadly ranch wife . . . uh uh. No thanks. We were doing fine in the . . .

What was that in his right hand? Little Alfred's right hand, that is. He appeared to be holding a strip of something white in his right hand, and he seemed to be more or less gesturing with it, pointing it in our direction.

41

I squinted my eyes, lifted my ears to Full Alert position, and gave my tail several slow whaps on the floor. The light was so poor out there that I could hardly . . . sniff sniff.

BACON?

A strip of raw bacon?

I sampled the air again to confirm my original reading on the alleged material, and . . . yes, the boy had come armed with a slice of raw bacon.

Oh brother.

Have we ever discussed raw bacon? Maybe not. It's not a subject I enjoy discussing. I mean, it's a subject I love to discuss, also to dream about and eat, but any discussion of raw bacon is bound to expose a certain . . . well, weakness, you might say, in my innermost fundamental . . .

Okay, let's cut to the bottom line. I have a terrible weakness for raw bacon. There it is. I've never been able to say no to a slice of raw bacon.

Holy smokes, just saying it makes my mouth water!

Little Alfred was well aware of my weakness for bacon and he had come to tempt me.

I had to resist. Hey, I had figgered out his little game, I knew what he was trying to pull (lure us into his bedroom), and I HAD TO BE STRONG.

I turned my nose toward the north wall, hoping

that might . . . but the fragrant little bacon waves followed my nose and filled them with . . .

My ears began to jump around. My eyelids quivered. The last three inches of my tail began to squirm around like a . . . I don't know, like something that didn't belong to the rest of my body.

My mouth was watering so hard that I found it necessary to lick my chops, and that was a bad sign. I mean, when a guy goes to licking his chops, it usually means . . .

NO! Stop that! Tail, lie still. Mouth, go dry. Ears, be still. Nose, sniff no more.

I tried counting sheep. I pretended that I was locked in a sealed bubble, a soap bubble, into which no smell could penetrate.

No luck.

I tried to concentrate on the most unpleasant subject I could imagine—Pete the Barncat. I saw his grinning face and heard his sniveling, whining voice. Pete would want me to surrender to the Bacon Urge, to be lured into the depths of the house, and to be caught in the act by Sally May.

It seemed to be working, the Pete deal. I disliked him so much that the mere thought of him made the mere thought of raw bacon totally . . . boy, that stuff smelled delicious!

I couldn't turn off my nose. What's a guy to do?

I mean, you've got this very sensitive high-tech sensory device sitting out there on the end of your snoot and it can pick up the scent of a fly three hundred yards away in the midst of a hurricane and most of the time that's good, but sometimes it works against you when . . .

The smell of that bacon was about to drive me bazooka!

I was trembling. The waterworks of my mouth were pumping away, I mean, we're talking about an artesian well flowing a hundred gallons a minute, and when a guy has a river running through his mouth, he's got to . . . lick his chops.

"Drover, wake up. This is an emergency." Much to my surprise, he sat straight up. "Thanks, pal. I really hate to bother you, but I need your help, perhaps more than at any time in my entire career."

"I smell bacon."

"Yes, and I don't have time to go into all the details, but we must stiffen our resolve and deny ourselves the momentary pleasure of . . . "

"Raw bacon?"

"Exactly. And as I was saying, this is going to be one of those deals where we have to operate on total blind trust."

"I see."

"So I guess it all comes down to this, Drover: Do

44

you trust me totally, or would you rather be struck blind for the rest of your life?"

"Oh my gosh!"

"I must confide in you, my friend. The smell of that bacon is pulling me, luring me, tugging me into Sally May's House of Horrors, from which no dog has ever returned alive."

"Oh my gosh!"

"And I'm depending on you to be strong, Drover. After years and years of being a dingbat, you must rise to the occasion and help me resist the lure of that bacon smell."

"Oh my gosh."

"We're depending on you, son, the entire amassed forces of the Security Division. If you weaken and crumble now, we'll all be thrashed by Sally May's broom, swept away like . . . I love bacon, Drover, stop me, do something, hurry!"

"Okay, Hank, I think I can handle it."

"I knew you could, Drover, honest I did. I always knew that somewhere in the garbage heap of your mind, there was a tiny bean sprout of courage, just waiting to grow into a mighty oak tree."

"I can do it, Hank. You can depend on me."

It was, to say the least, a touching moment. I mean, there we were, the elite of the Security Division, the cream of the tuna on toast. The smartest,

the strongest, the best in our profession. We were fighting for our dignity, our honor, our very survival, and why was Drover . . .

The moron, the dunce, the back-stabbing, two-timing, cheating, bushwhacking, counterfeit little . . . do you know what he did? *He marched over to Little Alfred and ate my bacon!*

Okay, so be it. This was war. Nobody eats MY bacon and lives to eat the second piece. Drover lived but he didn't eat the second piece—or did he? You'll see.

I love bacon.

C H A P T E R

6

THREE POUNDING HEARTS IN THE KITCHEN

I had to give Drover Growls and Fangs to convince him that I was taking charge of the case, but that was no big deal.

And then I had to follow Little Alfred into the kitchen to collect my bacon. He had come with only one piece, don't you see, and had to raid the friginator again.

Frigoriginator.

Figerator.

Phooey. The ice box.

He had to raid the ice box again to get my Special Bacon Award. Following the beam of his flashlight, we crept on silent toes and paws into the kitchen. There, we halted in front of the frigin . . . ice box.

Alfred put a finger to his lips and said, "Shhh." And he gave me a wink. I didn't wink back because, well, dogs don't wink.

Do we? I don't think so. Seems to me that our eyelids more or less work together, and where one goes the other is likely to follow.

Anyways, I didn't wink back but I did move my paws up and down, signaling Enormous Anticipation, and I did lick my chops and went to Broad Joyous Swings on the tail section.

I'm sure the boy knew at a glance that this was a very important moment in my career, and would you like to guess what the little stinkpot did?

Instead of just handing me the bacon or holding it out so that I could lift it gently from his outstretched fingers, he laid it over the top of my snout.

You can't imagine what a commotion this caused. I mean, there I was, dying inside from bacon lust, and he draped my award over the top of my snout—where I was getting extreme and maximum smells but where I couldn't reach it with my tongue and teeth.

I tried a correction manuever, moving my jaws at a high rate of speed—chomping, that is—but that didn't seem to help. I then shifted into a second correction maneuver: shot my tongue straight out to Max Length, threw a 180-degree curl into it, and sent it arcing back over the top of my nose.

Did you follow all of that? It was pretty complicated, actually, and if you missed some of the steps, don't worry. As long as I know what I'm doing, it doesn't matter if you do or not.

I definitely knew what I was doing and I did it about as well as it could be done. That Reverse Curl was pretty amazing but I ran out of tongue about half an inch short of the prize.

At that point, I initiated Correction Three: went to Full Reverse on all engines, in hopes that . . . well, the thought had occurred to me that if I ran backwards fast enough, my mouth might somehow catch up with the, uh, elusive bacon.

Not a bad idea but it didn't work either. What it did accomplish was to crash my tail section into a kitchen chair, which more or less scooted and scratched across the limoleun floor and caused all three of us to freeze in our tracks.

In the dead silence, we heard a bed squeak in a distant room. Then, a voice that sent cheers of fill down my spine, chills of fear, and we're talking about serious heavy-duty fills of cheer, because the voice belonged to the most feared woman on the ranch.

In all of Ochiltree County.

In the whole state of Texas.

Sally May.

Yes, it was her voice. She didn't have much to say at that hour of the night, but then Sally May didn't have to say a whole lot to scare the living bejeebers out of two dogs and one little boy.

She said, "Alfred?"

Dead silence, fellers, except for all the throbbing hearts in the room. Three throbbing hearts. Nobody breathed or moved. We were frozen, petrified . . . although that bacon was still draped over my snout and I found myself twisting my head around to see if I could . . .

You know, if a guy twists his head far enough in one direction, he'll fall over backwards. Try it some time. Just lean your head back as far as she'll go, and then lean it back some more. It works.

Boy, I felt pretty silly, falling over backwards right in the middle of such a scary scenery, but by George, it happened before I knew it.

Alfred almost had a stroke. His eyes were *this* big around . . . I guess you can't see how big around they were . . . his eyes got as big around as, I don't know, real big and real wide, and he had his finger up to his lips and he was trying to tell me to shut up and be still.

I froze. Alfred froze. Drover shivered. In the silence, we heard another dreaded squeak of the bed. Then, the dreaded voice: "Alfred? Is that you?"

Alfred's eyes flew from side to side. He didn't know what to do: answer, say nothing, stand still, or run like a striped ape. I sympathized because I didn't have a great plan for my own, uh, health and survival, shall we say.

And I was getting worried about Drover. You know Drover. When he gets scared, he just falls apart. He'll run in circles, squeak, crash into things. You never know what the little mutt's going to do next.

So far, he was holding himself together. That was good because we had pretty muchly drifted into one of those situations from which some dogs never return alive. I mean, if Sally May ever caught us in her kitchen in the middle of the . . .

Ooooo boy, we didn't need to go very far down that road to find a couple of tombstones.

How had I gotten myself into this mess? Oh yes, the storm. And the bacon, speaking of which . . . I still hadn't been able to snag that bacon and the aroma of it was about to drive me . . .

The Voice That Chills came again from the other room.

"Loper, wake up."

"Uuuuuu."

"Loper, somebody is in this house."

"Uuuuuuu a;ckeit cl0e89dskcgh slckbnbedn—3um."

"Loper, wake up!"

"Huh? What?"

"I heard a sound in the kitchen."

"I'll be derned."

"Would you like to go check it out?"

"Nope." Silence. "Ouch! Those are my ribs."

"Dear, please."

"Okay, okay. Okay." The bed squeaked. Footsteps on the floor. "Okay. Kitchen. All you people in the kitchen stand at attention. Here I come."

He was coming. That was pretty serious but not nearly as serious as if Sally May Herself had come. Somehow the thought of getting murdered by Loper didn't terrify me as much.

Still, we had to do something. I glanced at Alfred. He looked rather pale, seemed to me, and scared beyond recognition. The sound of bare feet moving across the floor filled the dreadful silence. They were coming our way.

The feet, that is. Loper was coming our way too, walking on his . . . you get the idea.

I was still watching Alfred, waiting for him to give us a sign. *Son, do something. Don't just stand there. Several lives are at stake here.*

The footsteps were coming closer and closer. My heart was pounding. The boy was frozen in his tracks. I was so scared that I could no longer smell that wonderful bacon draped over my snout. That's pretty scared.

Footsteps in the darkness.

The rumble of thunder outside.

Hearts racing and pounding.

Then . . .

7

INSIDE THE COVEROUS
CAVERN

At last he made his move, and not a second too late. Too soon, I guess it ought to be. He made his so-forth not a second too soon.

He darted through the nearest doorway and into his bedroom, which lay just to the south of the kitchen. That was a piece of good luck for us, that his room was close by.

Alfred didn't say a word to me or Drover about following him, but then again, he didn't need to say a word. I was ready to get out of there.

On silent paws that made not a sound, I brushed past Drover and whispered, "You stole my bacon, you little creep."

We whisked ourselves through the door and into Alfred's room. The boy oozed himself into his bed and, well, I guess he wanted us to crawl UNDER the bed, but in the excitement and confusion of the . . .

We jumped into bed with him, is more or less what we did, and went slithering beneath the covers, straight to the bottom. See, I'm not fond of the underneath-side of beds. Too many spiders.

And dust. Drover has allergies, don't forget, and the last thing we needed was for him to go into a fit of sneezing.

But back-to the spider deal, I'm no chicken liver but I don't get along with spiders. Don't laugh. We have a variety of spiders in this country called the Brown Fiddlebow and they're nothing to play around with.

They bite, don't you see, and they don't rattle or hiss before they bite. Rattlesnakes are bad enough but at least they give you some warning. Those spiders merely bite, and I've heard stories about what happens.

Your legs rot away. Your tail falls off. Your ears turn brown like autumn leaves and then they fall off too.

You want to crawl under a bed with a nest of Brown Fiddlebow spiders? Neither did I, and if Little Alfred didn't want two wet dogs under the covers with him, that was, as we say, too bad.

And besides the spiders and so forth, I like soft beds.

So there we were, under the covers and at the bottom of the bed, with Little Alfred's feet sticking in our faces. It was then and there, in the silence and in the darkness, that I came to a terrible realization.

"Drover," I whispered, "I've lost my bacon."

"Oh darn."

"And if you find it before I do, I would appreciate it if you would turn it in to the proper authorities."

"You bet."

"Because if you don't, if you steal another piece of my bacon, you little chiseler, your mother won't recognize your face when I get finished with it."

"Yeah, good old Mom. I wish she was here."

"If she were here, Drover, it would be very crowded."

"Oh, she didn't take up much space. They always said Mom was so thin, you couldn't see her if she turned sideways."

"Hmmm. That's very interesting."

"Yeah. And Uncle Spot always said she was too skinny to cast a shadow."

"I'll swan."

"They said she had worms."

"No kidding."

"And she didn't take the time to eat right."

"Uh huh."

"Too busy raising pups."

"Drover, did you hear anything I said about the bacon?"

"Oh yeah, she loved bacon. I'd almost forgotten how much she loved bacon."

"Drover, are you there?"

"Good old Mom. I wonder what she's doing today."

Sometimes . . . oh well. I had more serious matters to think about than Drover's mother, the poor woman. Just imagine the sleepless nights she'd spent, wondering what could have produced her feather-brained son.

Yes, I had very serious matters to think about, such as the footsteps that by this time had reached the kitchen. I lay perfectly still and listened.

The light switch clicked on.

"Hello?" said Loper. "Any ghosts around? Hon, nobody's here. You must have heard the storm."

"Check Alfred and make sure he's all right."

"Hon . . . "

"Please."

"Okay. Okay, I'll check Alfred. I don't have anything better to do at this hour of the . . . " His voice trailed off into silence. Then, "Hon, did you spill some water on the kitchen floor?"

"No, I didn't."

"That's funny, I just stepped in a puddle."

Upon hearing this, I turned to Drover. "Did you hear that?"

"What was it? Gosh, I hope it's not one of those monsters."

"It was Loper. He's in the kitchen and he stepped in a puddle of water. And I think I know where it came from."

"Yeah, all this rain and stuff."

"Not rain and stuff, Drover. You."

There was a moment of silence, and then I heard him sniffle. "Well, I was scared. I heard Sally May's voice and I thought she was going to come into the kitchen and find us and chase us with a butcher knife, and it scared me so bad . . . "

"Okay, okay. I knew you'd do something, I just didn't know what."

"Yeah, and I feel terrible about it."

"And don't forget that you ate my bacon. Little Alfred brought that first piece just for ME and you stole it."

"Oh, the guilt's just piling up! I'm not sure I can live with myself."

"Never mind, Drover. We'll take this up at another time—if we should happen to survive the night, that is."

"Oh my leg!"

"Shhhhh."

Where were we? Oh yes, Loper was in the kitchen and had just discovered the Mysterious Puddle—which wasn't so mysterious to those of us who knew Drover. And now he, Loper, that is, was making his way into Alfred's room.

If he turned on the light, we were sunk. I mean, two dogs under the covers in a little boy's bed make humps, right? If he turned on the light, he would see the humps, jerk off the covers, and we would be exposed for all the world to see.

The rest of what might follow was too scary to think about.

We held our breath and waited. Would he turn on the light? No, he didn't.

Going strictly on the sounds picked up by my ears, here's what I imagined that he did. He walked over to the bed and looked down. Alfred was asleep—or so it appeared. Loper straightened the covers and said, "Well, everybody's in bed except me, and what am I doing walking around in the middle of the night?"

He yawned and then . . . uh oh. He sniffed the air. "Smells like goats in here. We may need to haul some sneakers to the dump."

He yawned again and went back to bed. Back in the bedroom, I heard him say, "Hon, I think you were dreamin'. Everything's fine."

"Loper, I heard something, I know I did."

The bed squeaked. "Well, you can take the next patrol. I've got a date with a beautiful pillow. Night."

Silence. The sounds of Loper's snoring reached my ears, and at last I dared to breathe. Alfred's toe gouged me in the ribs and the next thing I knew, he was under the covers with us.

"Hi, doggies. We sure fooled my dad, didn't we? He thought I was asweep, and he didn't even know ya'll dogs were here."

Right. We lucked out, but there was no sense in pushing our luck. It was time for us to go back outside.

"We're in a cave, aren't we? You want to pway Expwore the Cave? Don't ya think that would be fun?"

Uh . . . no, we really needed to be going, but thanks anyway.

"It's still waining outside, and thundoo and wightning too, and I'm gwad we're all together in my bed. I was scared, but I'm not scared any-more. I've got my doggies wiff me."

Yes, that was touching, a boy and his dogs, but the other side of that particular coin was "a boy's MOTHER and his dogs," and that one gave me the creeps. We could fool Loper, but Sally May was another story.

She couldn't be fooled. She had eyes in the back of her head, ears that heard everything, a nose that could find a sugar ant in a ten-section pasture.

And worst of all, she was always suspicious. I mean, every time she came around me, she seemed to read my innermost thoughts, some of which . . . many of which . . . okay, most of which aroused her disapproval.

And if it was okay with everyone, I was ready to take my chances with the storm outside, now that we were fairly sure that it was just a storm and not an invasion of . . . I had never totally bought into that business of the Little Green Monsters anyway.

"So you weckon I ought to wet you back outside?"

Uh huh. Yes. That was the best idea, in and out with no major bloodshed.

The boy heaved a sigh. "Well, all wight. Come on and we'll sneak ya'll back outside."

Whew!

All three of us crawled out of the coverous cavern. Once outside the sheets, I turned to Drover and was about to tell him to hurry up when I heard . . .

Smack, smack, gulp.

I froze and sniffed the air. All at once I caught the smell of . . .

G.L.Holmes

CHAPTER

8

A MYSTERIOUS
PHONE CALL

I sniffed the air again, just to be sure.

"Drover, all at once I smell bacon."

"Yeah, me too. I wonder what it could be."

"I think it could be bacon, Drover, because bacon smells exactly like bacon."

"Yeah, I've noticed that too. Funny how that happens."

"You won't think it's so funny if I find out that you ate my property. Did you just eat some bacon?"

"Well, let's see here. Yes, I did but I'm pretty sure it wasn't yours. It was just lying around under the covers. I don't think it belonged to anybody. It was lost."

I felt my temper rising. *"It was lost?* What kind of clam-brained answer is that? You knew exactly whose bacon that was and you ate it anyway."

"Well, I thought . . . "

"You'll pay for this, Drover. If we ever get out of this house alive, you will pay a terrible price for your greed and gluttony and stealing from your very best friend in the whole world. How can you stand yourself?"

"I don't know. I smell pretty bad when I'm wet."

"That smell comes from your rotten sense of morals, Drover. Who would steal two slices of bacon from his best friend?"

"Well, let's see. Pete would."

"Yes, of course, but he's a cat. Is that your standard of behavior? Do you want to be a cat when you grow up?"

"Not really."

"Well, you just might, pal. Were you aware that researchers have found a direct link between bacon and cats?"

"No, I missed that."

"They've found—and this is a laboratory test, Drover, solid scientific evidence—they've found that dogs who eat two or more slices of bacon often *turn into cats*."

"Oh my gosh!"

"And the group with the highest risk included dogs with sawed-off stub tails."

"Oh my gosh!"

"Yes. You're sorry now, aren't you? Huh? You may have just thrown your whole life away, Drover, and for what?"

"I don't want be a cat. I don't even like cats. I'd hate myself if I turned into a cat."

"Well, that may be your punishment, son. I'm sorry."

"You couldn't help it."

"Thanks. Let's get out of here."

Little Alfred was already down on the floor and creeping towards the kitchen. I smothered my anger and outrage, hopped off the bed, and followed him through the gloomy darkness.

We sneaked our way through the bedroom and into the kitchen. In the middle of the kitchen, Little Alfred stopped, placed a finger over his lips, and said, "Shhh."

I don't know why he felt the need to tell us to shush. We were operating in Stealthy Crouch Mode and couldn't have moved any silenter if we'd been flies wearing . . . something. Ballet slippers, I suppose.

But he stopped in the middle of the kitchen—Alfred did—and gave us the shush signal, and then we began the last leg of our dangerous journey to the back door.

We had gone no more than two or three steps when, suddenly and all of a sudden, the creepy dark silence of the night was ripped and torn by the loud ring of a bell.

Holy smokes, we must have tripped a fire alarm . . . burglar alarm . . . air raid siren . . . whatever . . . something that made a terrible loud ringing sound. And fellers, you talk about having the liver scared right out of you! That did it.

All at once, we had chaos amongst the yearlings, so to speak. I mean, it was totally dark in there except for the eerie flashes of lightning coming through the windows, and children and dogs were running in all directions.

In the space of ten seconds, I ran into Drover three times. I don't know where he was going. He didn't know where he was going. Running in circles, I suppose.

Then Little Alfred stampeded right over the top of me, stepped on my tail in two places, and went streaking back to his bed.

The Thing, the awful Ringing Thing, rang a second time, sending another jolt of electrical fear down my spine and out to the end of my tail. I had lost all sense of direction. I banged my nose into the kitchen cabinets, slipped and slided on the limoleun floor, and continued to stumble over Drover.

It was then that I began to piece together the pieces of the puzzle. The ringing we had heard, the awful piercing ring that had thrown us into such a panic turned out to be . . .

Hmmm, the telephone, it seemed.

The phone was ringing, don't you see, and that would have been no big deal except for one small detail. Sally May jumped out of bed and came pounding through the house in our direction.

Why? Because the telephone happened to be mounted on the kitchen wall, the east wall to be exact, and since that's where the telephone was ringing . . . you get the point.

Here she came. BAM, BAM, BAM. Those were her footsteps on the floor. As far as I knew, Sally May had a fairly dainty set of hooves, but they sure didn't sound dainty at that hour of the night, when she was chasing the telephone.

Shook the whole house, is what she did, and you can imagine the effect this had on me and Drover . . . mostly Drover. It threw us . . . him . . . into a new and higher dimension of terror.

I mean, from the moment we had set foot in this house, the thing we had feared most was a face-to-face meeting with Sally May.

And now SHE WAS COMING OUR WAY, sounding like thirteen Frankincense Monsters or a herd of charging elephants, and there we were in the middle of her kitchen, running around in circles and banging into things and wondering what form of execution she would choose for us.

Hanging?

Firing squad?

Flogging to death with a broom?

Strangulation?

Perhaps you're wondering why we didn't do the obvious and simple thing, follow Alfred into his room and seek shelter in his closet or beneath his bed.

It wasn't fear of spiders, I can tell you that. The thought of standing before Sally May's frigid glare caused my fear of spiders to melt away like . . . something.

Butter on a piece of corn. A snowflake on a branding iron.

Give me ten thousand crawling spiders and I'll shake all eight hands of all ten thousand if it will spare me the fate of being caught in the house by Sally May.

Trouble was, we couldn't find our way to Alfred's room. I mean, it was very dark in there, and after a guy runs in circles for a while, he loses all sense of direction.

And she was almost there and we were almost dead meat, but at the last possible second, I squirted myself beneath the kitchen table and poured myself into a ball in the corner, as far away from her as I could get.

Which wasn't nearly far enough but the best I could do.

Drover followed.

There, we ceased all breathing and waited to see what would happen. Here's what happened.

First, she switched on the light—not once but several times—and nothing happened. I mean, no light came on. It appeared that the storm had knocked out the electricity.

Second, the phone continued to ring—a third ring, then a fourth—until at last she found the receiver.

Then, in a sleepy voice, she said, "Hello? Who is this? Do you know what time it is? Uh huh. Then what . . . oh. Ohhhhhh. Oh my goodness. Yes, right away. I hope you'll be all right, and thanks for calling."

She hung up the phone. By this time, Loper had gotten up and wandered out into the middle of the house, somewhere close to where Sally May was located.

His voice sounded pretty croaky. "Now what? This place is like trying to sleep in downtown Amarillo."

"That was Slim. He just got a call from the sheriff's office in town. We're under a tornado warning. There's one on the ground and heading our way. Everyone on the creek is supposed to take cover."

"Wow, that woke me up. Okay, hon, we'd better head for the cellar. You grab Molly and a blanket. Where's the flashlight?"

"In the top drawer, where it's supposed to be."

Loper's feet shuffled across the kitchen floor. "Dadgum, there's that water again." He opened the drawer and felt around inside. "Hon, it's gone."

"It was there just yesterday."

"It's gone now."

"I'm not ABOUT to go into that musty cellar without a flashlight. There's no telling what might be down there."

Just then, guess who came out of his bedroom, walking in the beam of the missing flashlight.

"Hi, Mom. Hi, Dad. Are ya wooking for the fwashwight?"

There was a moment of silence. Then, Loper said, "Why, yes, we were, and one of these days I'd like to hear the story of how you happen to be walking around in the middle of the night with it, but not now."

Loper took the flashlight and started giving orders. Alfred was to get his blankie and pillow. (In Kid Language, "blankie" means blanket.) Sally May was to gather up Baby Molly while he, Loper, would open several windows and dig a couple of raincoats out of the closet. And everyone was supposed to wear shoes, since they would be walking across weeds and stickers, plus waterdogs, snakes, lizards, and whatever else might be lurking in the darkness.

Moments later, they had all gathered in the kitchen. From my hiding place under the table, I could see their feet and ankles. (The flashlight was on, see.)

Loper spoke in a voice that was soft but firm. "Everybody here? When we get outside, join hands and stay together. Let's go, ya'll."

And with that, they left the house and went out into the stormy night. The last thing I heard before the door closed behind them was Sally May's comment, "What on earth happened to my screen door! Just wait 'til I get hold of those dogs!"

Gulp.

Oh yes, and then Little Alfred whispered, "Bye, doggies. Good wuck."

Good wuck indeed. We would need several truckloads of it.

C H A P T E R

9

WE HEAR THE ROAR OF THE HURRICANE

They were gone. We were left alone in the eerie silence of the house. Off in another room, I could hear a clock ticking.

I hoped it was a clock ticking. If it wasn't a clock, then it was something worse, and right then I didn't want to speculate on what it might be.

I mean, when a guy finds himself alone in a big empty house, he begins to hear odd little sounds and his imagination starts playing tricks on him.

We sure didn't need any of that. Our deal was looking bad enough without any extras.

I moved myself out from under the table, out into the middle of the kitchen floor, and began pacing. My mind seems to work better when I pace. Have I ever mentioned that? Maybe not.

I began pacing. "Well, Drover, this situation has gone from bad to worse. First, we got ourselves lured into the house by a bratty little boy. Then we almost got caught. And now we've been abandoned in the midst of a storm."

"Yeah, and I'm fixing to turn into a cat!"

I stopped pacing. "What?"

"I'm fixing to turn into a cat. I can feel it happening already, 'cause I feel more like I do right now than I did a while ago."

"What are you talking about?"

"You said I was going to turn into a cat 'cause I ate your bacon. And I think it's starting to happen."

"Oh, that. Forget it, Drover, we've got much bigger problems to think about."

He was starting to cry. "My mom's going to be so disappointed! The last thing she said when I left home was, 'Drover, be a good little dog.' She never wanted a cat for a son, and now look what I've done!"

"I tried to warn you."

"I know you did. You've been a good friend and I wish I'd never tasted raw bacon."

"Yes, it's almost ruined you. On the other hand, we might try the cure."

"The cure?" He came padding out from under the table. "You mean . . . "

"Exactly. The same team of brilliant scientists who discovered the link between bacon and Cattination, those same guys came up with a cure. Didn't I mention that?"

"No, I didn't know about it." He began hopping up and down. "Oh Hank, tell me about it, let me be cured. I'll be a good dog for the rest of my life, honest I will!"

"Hmmm." I paced a few steps away, paused a moment to think, then turned back to Drover. "Okay, I'll do it, just this once and not because you deserve it, because you don't."

"I know. I was a rat."

"You really were, Drover."

"And a pig. I was a terrible pig for hogging all the bacon. I was a pig-hog."

"You certainly were."

"But that's all behind me now. No more bacon for me. I'm a changed dog."

"I'm glad to hear that, son. It renews my hope in . . . you know, we really don't have time to discuss your personal problems."

"Oh my gosh. What are we going to do?"

"I'm not sure. I was hoping you might have some ideas."

"Well, let's get me cured, before I turn into a cat."

"Oh yes, the cure. Here's the deal. Roll over three times and repeat the, uh, curative words. Let's see,

> Piggy bacon, wrongly taken.
>
> Piggy ways are now forsaken.

"I think I can do it, Hank! Watch this." He rolled over three times and said the, uh, magic curative words. Then he leaped to his feet and gave himself a shake. "There, I did it and I'm so happy! I don't feel like a cat any more."

"Great, Drover, I'm happy for you. Oh, one last part of the cure: I get all the supper scraps for a week."

"Sure, Hank, that's the least I can do."

He hopped and skipped with joy. I watched him and felt a glow of, well, fatherly pleasure, you might say. Helping others through difficult situations has always . . .

Huh? All at once my thoughts were pulled away from good deeds and helping others, as I suddenly realized that (a) the wind had stopped blowing; (b) the rain had stopped falling; (c) the air seemed thick and heavy.

A spooky calmness had moved through the house, across the ranch, perhaps across the entire world.

"Drover, do you notice anything odd?"

"Well, let's see. We're dogs and we're in the house where the people stay, but all the people went outside where the dogs stay. That seems kind of odd to me."

"Yes, but I mean the air."

"Oh." He sniffed the air. "Yeah, it smells like two wet dogs and I guess that's odd."

"Wrong again, Drover. All at once the air is still and heavy, and those are symptoms of a hurricane. Are you familiar with hurricanes?"

"I thought they said 'tornado.'"

"No, a tornado has never struck this valley. We've already discussed that. It must be a hurricane. Do you know about hurricanes?"

"Well . . . not really"

"A huge swirling wind, Drover, one of the most destructive storms in all of nature. It can pick up trees, cars, houses, even dogs, and carry them to who-knows-where."

Lightning twinkled outside and in its spooky silver light I saw Drover's eyes. They had grown to the size of pies.

"Oh my gosh, I had just started feeling safe 'cause Sally May left the house, but now you're telling me . . . "

"I'm telling you that hurricanes are even more dangerous than Sally May when she's mad."

"Oh my gosh!"

"And we're in grave danger."

"Oh, this leg is killing me!"

My teeth were beginning to chatter. My legs were quivering. The air was so heavy now, I could hardly breathe. "Drover, we've got to get out of here. But how?"

"Yeah, but how?"

"Good question."

"Thanks."

"You're welcome."

I found myself pacing again, as I tried to focus all my powers of concentration on this problem which seemed to have no solution. I mean, we were locked inside a house, right?

I thought and thought and thought, and also paced and paced and paced. Nothing. It wasn't working.

"Drover, we're cooked."

"Yeah, and I'm not even hungry."

I stopped pacing and whirled around to face him. "Yes, because you ate two pieces of my bacon, you little sneak, and . . . why did you mention food? I was talking about something else."

"Well, I don't know. I guess I'm so scared, I'm liable to say anything. I think you said something about . . . somebody was cooking supper . . . I think."

"Hmmm. That doesn't ring any bells."

Suddenly a bell rang . . . the telephone again, perhaps the sheriff's department calling to . . .

Drover jumped. "Oh my gosh, there's one now!"

"Yes, and it's all come back to me. I had just said, 'We're cooked, Drover,' because we are now trapped between Sally May and a deadly swirling hurricane."

"Oh my gosh, oh my leg, I'm going to jump out a window and get out of here!"

He left the kitchen and went streaking into the living room. "I'm afraid that won't work, Drover. We would be cut to pieces on the glass, so I'd advise you not to . . . "

I heard a thump, then . . . his voice. "I did it, Hank, I made it through the window and now I'm outside!"

I hurried into the living room, towards the sound of his voice. "That's impossible, Drover. I didn't hear the crash of broken glass. You see, windows are made of window glass, therefore . . . "

"Yeah, but the window was open and I knocked the screen off and here I am, outside. Are you proud of me?"

Hmmmm. It appeared that this thing needed, uh, further study. I went streaking to the so-called window and found . . . by George, there was an open window in the living room, and it appeared that someone or something had . . . well, removed the screen, so to speak.

"Okay, Drover, relax. The pieces of the puzzle are falling into place. You're probably wondering why that window happened to be open, aren't you?"

"Not really."

"I mean, why would anyone open a window in the midst of a rainstorm? Most dogs would never figger that one out, Drover, but I happen to know the answer."

"You may know the answer but I'm outside the house."

"Hush, Drover, I'm about to tie this all together. You see, Loper opened several windows. That's what you're supposed to do when a hurricane is coming. Can you tell me why?"

"Hank, these clouds look awful. They're green."

"Let me finish. When a hurricane is coming, Drover, you open one window to let it in and a second window to let it out. That's why Loper opened the windows, don't you see, and that explains why .

"Hank, I hear something roaring."

"Huh? Roaring, you say?"

"Yeah." We were quiet for a moment, and . . . by George, I seemed to hear a certain . . . well, roaring sound. "Hank, do hurricanes bark or growl?"

"I don't think so. In other words, no."

"Do they roar?"

That roar was getting LOUDER.

"Drover, we may need to cut this lesson short and . . . yikes, maybe I'd better get out of here!"

And with that, I went flying through the open window.

C H A P T E R

10

OKAY, MAYBE IT WAS A TORNADO

You're probably wondering why Little Alfred had parked his stupid tricycle right under that window. I wondered that myself.

It was very careless of him. I mean, suppose the house had caught fire and members of his family had been jumping out the windows. Someone might have landed smack in the middle of his stupid two-bit tricycle, just as I did, and gotten a handlebar in the rib cage, just as I did.

Did it hurt? You bet it did.

Kids are supposed to park their tricycles on the porch, not under windows and fire escapes and emergency exits, but the most annoying part of this was that Drover had jumped out the same window only seconds before and . . .

How do you explain that?

He's so lucky, he doesn't need brains.

I limped around for a moment, trying to jump-start my hearts and lung. It was that serious. At last, I got 'em going again and turned a steely gaze on Mister Ate My Bacon.

"You might have warned me that I was about to dive into the middle of a killer tricycle!"

G.L.Holmes

"Well, I was so worried about the hurricane that I didn't think about it."

I stuck my nose right in his face. "Drover, if a dog gets killed on a tricycle, he doesn't need to worry about a hurricane, does he?"

"I never thought about that."

"Well, think about it. The answer is no."

"No what?"

"No. Just plain ordinary NO. That is the answer."

"Yeah, but I forgot the question."

Hmmmm. I too had forgotten the question, and all at once it didn't seem terribly important anyway, so . . . phooey.

Suddenly I heard something in the distance. I cocked one ear and listened. "Shhhh. Do you hear something?"

"Yeah, it's that same roar."

"Ah yes, the roar. It's quite a loud roar, isn't it?"

"Yeah. You don't reckon it's a train, do you?"

"I don't think so, Drover. I've never seen a train on this ranch."

"Slim trains horses."

"Good point. Maybe we'd better run up to the top of the hill and check it out."

And so it was that we left the yard, climbed over the fence, and went streaking out into the home pasture, until we reached a spot some fifty years north of the machine shed.

Yards, I should say, fifty yards. There, we were away from trees and buildings and other objects that blocked our view, and we established a Forward Observation Post.

Right away, we put our tail-ends together and began scanning the surrounding country. I surveyed the country east of us, while Drover took the western side.

"All right, Drover, tell me what you see."

"Well . . . it's awful dark."

"That checks out. Go on."

"I see . . . a lot of darkness, and some lightning, but more darkness than lightning."

"Exactly. Same over here. Any sign of a train?"

"Nope, no trains."

"Hmmm, yes, same over here. But I still hear that roaring noise. How about you?"

He cocked his ear and listened. "Yeah, there it is, off to the southwest, and it's getting louder."

"Right. We're getting the same readings on my end. Any sign of Loper and Sally May?"

"Nope. I don't see anyone, but I'm not surprised 'cause they went somewhere to make a big cattle trade."

I was silent for a moment, as I ran that comment through my data banks. "Cattle trade? I don't know what you mean."

"Well, the phone rang, remember? And then they all left the house, remember? And Loper said they were going to talk to the seller, and I just . . . "

"One moment, Drover. You assumed that this guy was trying to sell them some cattle, but I must warn you that we deal in facts, not assumptions."

"Oh darn, I goofed again."

"Yes, but don't get discouraged. You were right about the 'seller' part, so let's go back to that clue and see if we can pick up the trail."

"Okay, but I wonder what that funnel-looking thing is over there."

"The one clue we have is (a) a mysterious phone call in the middle of the night; and (b) an equally mysterious salesman who was selling something."

"It looks pretty big."

"Actually, Drover, we have two clues, not one, so things are moving right along. We'll have this little mystery knocked out in no time at all."

"Gosh, that thing looks green."

"Everything greens up after a rain, son, the grass, the trees . . . "

"I don't think it's a tree."

"Well, what do you expect? Everything can't be a tree. If everything were a tree, we'd have no dogs. Now, as I was saying, we have a salesman, calling in the middle of the night, and the question we must answer is this: What was he selling?"

"A funnel?"

"Don't be absurd. Nobody sells funnels in the middle of the night, and besides, you've already guessed cattle."

"Yeah, but . . . "

"Don't argue with me. You guessed cattle, and the point I'm trying to make, if you will just shut your little trap and listen, the point I'm trying to impress upon you . . . "

"Hank, that thing's moving this way."

"Hush, I'm just about to wrap this thing up. You supposed and assumed that he was selling *cattle* . . . "

"It's a funnel."

"All right, have it your way. You insist that he was selling funnels but he might just as well have been selling watermelons or horse feed, fence posts or barbed wire."

"Hank, I'm getting scared."

"Never fear the truth, Drover, even when it proves you wrong. Nothing is truer than the truth

. . . and that roar seems to be getting louder and louder, doesn't it?"

"Yeah, and that big black funnel is coming closer and closer."

"What? Speak up. I can't hear you over the roar . . . the wind seems to be picking up all of a sudden, doesn't it?"

"Hank, that thing doesn't look natural. It's HUGE!"

"What 'thing' are we talking about?"

"Turn around and look over this way."

Just to humor the little mutt, I turned around and did a quick scan of the Western Quadrant. "I see nothing, Drover, nothing but darkness and . . . " A spear of lightning cut across the dark sky and . . .

HUH?

"My goodness, what is that thing? It looks like a . . . well, a huge black funnel, you might say."

"That's what I was trying to tell you."

"Sometimes you have trouble communicating, Drover, and . . . all at once the pieces of the puzzle are coming together. Loper wasn't talking to a salesman. He was referring to the CELLAR, going to the cellar! And that fits in perfectly with all the talk about tornadoes, don't you see?"

"I thought it was a hurricane."

"We were misquoted, Drover, it happens all the time. Yes! The cellar, the roaring sound, the funnel . . . it's all fitting together, like a great big patchwork quilt. We've solved the mystery, Drover. There's a tornado running loose, and I guess you know what that means."

"Yeah, it's fixing to run over us."

"Exactly, unless we stiffen our backs, stand our ground, and bark as we've never barked before!"

"Oh my leg!"

"Don't squeak. Bark! Throw your whole body and soul into it. This one is for the ranch, Drover, so give it your best shot. Ready? Commence Heavy Duty Barking!"

Boy, you should have seen us! Standing alone on that windswept hill, we turned to face the charge of the Deadly Swirling Hurricane . . . Tornado, that is, just as I had suspected all along.

Yes, a terrible tornado. We snarled and snapped. We lunged and growled.

Was I scared? Not a bit. There's something about the excitement of combat that brings out hidden reserves of courage in a dog. The more you bark, the more you want to bark. The harder you fight, the harder you want to . . .

Okay, maybe we began to feel a little uneasy when the Thing didn't turn and run. I mean, we'd given it some pretty stern barking and . . . gulp . . . it should have stopped or . . . paused or . . . gulp . . . at least slowed down a little bit.

But it kept coming closer and closer and . . . you know, that Thing was turning out to be a whole lot bigger than I had . . . we're talking BIG like nothing I had ever seen before.

Hey fellers, that Thing wasn't just as big as a house, it was as big as the whole horse pasture . . . it was as big as a whole entire mountain! It was . . .

It was time for us to abandon ship, retreat, and get our little selves out of . . .

C H A P T E R

11

STRANGE CREATURES IN THE TORNADO

You want some good friendly advice? The next time you get a chance to bark at a tornado, go bark at a pickup.

Tornadoes, we discovered, pay exactly zero attention to barking dogs, even your finest top-of-the-line, blue-ribbon cowdogs.

So what happened? You're probably sitting on the edge of your chair, biting your toenails, and wondering what became of us two heroic guard dogs.

Well, we didn't succeed in stopping the tornado, but our barking did seem to alter its course. It missed headquarters, but I'm sorry to report that it didn't miss us.

All at once, it was upon us—this huge swirling Thing, this towering column of meanness and violence—all at once it was upon us. I shouted the order to retreat, but by then it was too late.

All around us things were lifting off the ground and flying through the air—dust, sprigs of grass, weeds, straw, and two dogs. Yes, although we tried to make a run for safety, we were swept up into the center of the storm.

Have you ever seen Sally May catch flies with her vacuum sweeper? Maybe not, but I have. Sometimes she'll find a bunch of noisy flies around her windows, and instead of smashing them (which is fun but creates a mess that has to be cleaned up), she goes for her vacuum sweeper and sucks 'em down the hose.

Pretty clever idea, but the point is that the tornado did pretty muchly the same thing to me and Drover. And all at once we were airborne, whizzing through the air and seeing a whole bunch of things you'd never expect to see whizzing through the air.

Things such as: the head and fan of an Aermotor windmill; three galvanized stock tanks; a sixteen-foot stock trailer; a boy's bicycle; three utility poles that had been broken off like matchsticks; a dozen chickens; several cottonwood trees; and two buzzards.

That's correct, two buzzards. They were sitting on a limb of one of the cottonwood trees and . . .

well, here was the conversation that unfolded. It was pretty strange. They were just waking up, don't you see, and Wallace was the first to notice us.

"Son? Junior? You'd best wake up, son, I'm a-seeing some strange things in the air."

"W-w-what?"

"I said wake up, Junior, 'cause all at once and for no good reason, I'm a-seeing dogs flying around our tree."

"D-d-d-dogs? Is that w-w-what you s-s-said, P-pa?"

"That's right, son. Two dogs are a-flying around this tree right this very moment, even as we speak."

"Oh, y-y-y-you're just d-d-dreaming, Pa. G-g-go back to s-s-s-sleep, back to sleep."

"I ain't dreaming, Junior, there are two dogs a-swooping around this tree, now you open your eyes and wake up, do you hear me?"

"Oh d-d-darn. I j-just got to s-s-s-s-sleep, and n-now you're w-w-waking m-me up." Junior lifted his ugly buzzard head off his chest, opened his eyes, and stared at us. "Oh m-m-my g-g-g-goodness!"

"Do you see 'em, son? Do you see them two dogs right out there in front of our tree? Tell me you do, son, because otherwise I'm having terrible hallusitanias."

"Oh m-my g-g-goodness, y-yes, I s-s-see 'em."

"Two dogs? You see 'em? Oh praise the Lord, I thought I'd lost my marbles, sure 'nuff."

"Y-y-yep, t-two d-d-dogs f-flying around our t-t-tree, P-pa, j-j-just like you s-s-said, like you said."

Wallace craned his neck and stared at us for a long time. "Now Junior, the next question is this: How on earth can two dogs be a-flying around our tree, is the next question."

"W-w-well, l-let me th-think. M-maybe they're b-b-bird dogs."

"I don't think bird dogs fly, son. Bird dogs hunt birds, is what they do, but they don't fly, and them two dogs are flyin', sure 'nuff. What do you reckon is going on here?"

"W-w-well, it b-b-beats me, but one of th-them is our d-d-doggie friend." He waved his wing, 'Hi, d-d-doggie.' "And m-m-maybe we could, uh, ask him."

"Good thinkin', son. I'll do the talkin'." Wallace puffed himself up and gave us a hateful glare. "What are ya'll dogs doing, lurkin' around our tree in the middle of the night like a couple of I-don't-know-whats? This here's our cottonwood tree, it's our buzzard roost, and ya'll have no business being here, but since you are, what are you doing here and I never knew that dogs could fly."

Whilst Drover was dog-paddling through the air and trying to figure how to limp when there was no ground underfoot—whilst he was busy with other matters, I turned my attention to the buzzards.

"Evening, Junior. Howdy, Wallace."

"Don't you howdy-Wallace me, pooch, just answer the question. What's a-going on around here?"

"Well, Wallace, it seems that the four of us have gotten involved in a tornado." No response from the buzzards. "Hello? Anybody home? Tor-na-do. A powerful storm that can pick up dogs and buzzards and send them flying through the air."

"Pooch, if I want a weather report, I'll ask a groundhog. What are you a-doing around our tree, is what I want to know."

"I told you, you bird-brain. We've all been swept up in a tornado."

Wallace glared at me. "Dog, that is one of the most ignert things I ever heard. In case you didn't notice, we're a-roosting in our cottonwood tree."

"Yeah, well, your cottonwood tree is flying around in a tornado, and you just happen to be attached to it."

"It ain't."

"It sure as thunder is, and if you don't believe me . . . " Just then a milk cow floated past. "If you don't believe me, then maybe you'd like to talk about flying milk cows."

Wallace's eyes popped open and his beak dropped about six inches. Then he shook his head in disgust and turned back to Junior.

"Son, you talk to him. I can't understand what that dog's trying to say. Something about a storm somewhere."

"W-w-well, I think h-he s-said w-we got s-swooped up in a t-t-t-t . . . storm, a tornado storm."

"A tornado? Do you mean a cyclone, a terrible swirling storm?"

"Y-yeah, only it's c-c-called a t-t-tornado, tornado, P-pa."

"It ain't. It's called a cyclone. That's what my daddy called it. That's what my granddaddy called it, and that's what it IS—a cyclone."

"W-w-well, whatever, Pa. C-cyclone or t-t-t-tornado, w-w-w-we're in the m-m-middle of one that p-p-pulled up our r-r-roosting tree."

The old man's eyes darted from me and back to Junior. "Well, why didn't he just say so?"

"I th-think he d-d-did, Pa."

"No, he never. He was jabbering about . . . I don't know what-all. Groundhogs and milk cows, and furthermore . . . " He whirled around and faced me again. "And furthermore, puppy, I have lived on this earth for a long time and I've never been swooped up in a cyclone before, never even seen one, and . . . " Back to Junior. "Son, do you reckon we really are in a cyclone?"

"W-w-well, I d-don't s-see any g-g-ground under our t-t-t-tree, d-d-do you?"

Wallace looked down. "No, I most certainly don't, and son, I told you there was something bad in them clouds and we needed to watch 'em close."

"Y-y-you d-did not."

"Did too."

"D-d-d-did n-not, 'cause y-y-you f-f-fell right off to s-s-sleep, to sleep."

"Well, I meant to. It sure crossed my mind, and if I didn't exactly say it, I sure . . . " He whirled around to me. "All right, dog, maybe you ain't as crazy as I thought."

"Gee, thanks, Wallace. Sometimes you say the nicest things."

"But don't let it go to your head. The point is, if we're all flyin' around inside a cyclone, what do we do next?"

"To be real honest about it, I don't know. This is my first one. I guess we could sing."

His eyes widened and his beak twisted into an ugly snarl. "Sing! Why, that's the ignertest thing you've said since the last ignert thing you said. Singin' never helped anybody survive a cyclone, and besides all that, I don't like music, never have."

G.L. Holmes

Junior's face broke into a big smile. "Y-y-yeah, but I j-just love to s-s-s-sing, P-pa." He turned to me. "W-w-we'd j-just l-love to s-s-sing, love to sing, d-d-doggie."

Wallace grumbled to himself and turned his back on us. "We would not. It'll be a cold snowy day in Brownsville when I sing with a dog, for crying out loud, in the middle of a cyclone! I never heard of such an ignert thing."

"Oh c-c-c-come on, P-pa, d-d-don't be s-such a g-g-grouch, such a grouch."

"I am a grouch, I'm proud to be a grouch, and I plan to be a grouch for the rest of my life, and anybody who don't like it can go sit on a great big tack, is what he can do."

By then, I had come up with a compromise solution. "Tell you what, Wallace, the song I have in mind has four parts, so we need your voice. But you don't have to sing pretty. You sing grouchy and we'll sing pretty."

He whirled around. "Now, I might go for a deal like that, but I ain't going to sing pretty or even try to sing pretty, because I ain't a dainty little warbler . . . " He whirled back to Junior. "And neither are you, son, and you'd best remember who you are. We're buzzards, son."

"Uh okay, P-pa."

"And buzzards ain't warblers or little hummingbirds."

"F-f-fine, P-pa."

"Buzzards is buzzards, and we're proud of our Buzzardhood, and buzzards never sing pretty."

"Uh okay, f-f-fine, y-you b-b-bet, P-pa. S-s-start the s-s-song, d-d-doggie."

And with that . . . well, you'll see.

12

WOW, WHAT A GREAT ENDING!

You ever sing the kind of song that's called a "round"?

It's a song that . . . hmmm, that's kind of hard to describe, come to think of it. Everybody sings the same verse, don't you see, but they come in at different times and somehow it all fits together.

Examples? Okay, "Three Blind Mice" is one, and so is "Row, Row, Row Your Boat," and so is "Why Doesn't My Goose Sing As Well As Thy Goose." And I'll bet that at some time in your life, you've sung one of those songs as a round.

And that's what we did, only we spiffed it up. See, we started off singing "Why Doesn't My Goose" as a round. Then we split up and each of us took a different song and we sang them ALL as a round, at the same time.

Pretty impressive, huh? You bet it was. Old Mister Sour Puss took the "Goose" song, Junior took "Row Your Boat," and Drover took "Three Blind Mice."

Never in all of history had two dogs and two buzzards attempted such an amazing musical fiasco in the middle of a tornado.

Furthermore, whilst the other three guys were singing the other three songs in a round, I contributed snippets from . . . you'll never guess and boy, will you be surprised . . .

. . . from the "Hallelulia Chorus."

I told you you'd be shocked, stunned, speechless, impressed beyond description, and sure enough, you were.

You should have heard it. In fact, you ought to hear it. It's on the cassette tape version of this story.

Anyways, it turned out to be a total knock-out song and we were all thrilled with it . . . everyone but Wallace, that is, who was determined to be unthrilled and unimpressed, but nobody cared what he thought anyway.

We might have kept right on singing but for one small detail that you probably forgot: We were taking a ride on a runaway tornado, and all at once . . . something changed.

Maybe the winds slacked off. Maybe the tornado went up or down. Maybe the tornado didn't like our music. But something happened, and the next thing we knew, the tornado had spit us out, so to speak, and we found ourselves, all four of us, blown into the topmost branches of a huge cottonwood tree.

And this was a normal cottonwood, the kind with its roots in the ground on Planet Earth. The tornado went roaring away, and suddenly we found ourselves surrounded by total silence.

Wallace broke the silence with his hacksaw voice. "Junior, where are we at?"

"W-w-well, I d-don't know, P-pa, but I th-think w-w-w-we're out of the t-t-t-tornado, th-thank g-g-goodness."

"It was a cyclone, son."

"T-t-tornado."

"Cyclone."

"T-t-t-tornado."

"Son, it was a cyclone but never mind because we have survived, which is wonderful news, but I wonder if them two dogs might have suffered a . . . you know, we ain't had full grub in several days,

Junior, and why don't we check on our buddies and see."

"Sorry, Wallace," I said. "We're over here and doing fine, and we sure appreciate your concern."

He heaved a sigh and gave his head a shake. "A buzzard is always an optimist and that's why we get our hearts broke so many times. All right, Junior, we've had all the fun I can stand, it's time to get airborne and hunt grub."

"It was fun, Wallace."

"Fun for you, puppy dog, 'cause you've got nothing better to do than to goof off and sing silly songs, but we buzzards get paid by the job, yes we do, and no workie, no eat. Come on, Junior, my belly button's rubbin' a hole in my backbone."

He pushed himself off the limb and went flapping off into the darkness. Junior grinned and waved a wing goodbye and said, "W-w-well, s-s-see you n-next t-t-time, d-d-doggie." And then he flew away, leaving Drover and me alone with our thoughts—and with a pretty serious problem.

See, you might have thought our story had reached a happy ending, but that's not the case. Yes, we had just ridden a wild bucking tornado completely into the ground, and yes, we had even managed to spend a couple of hours in Sally May's house without getting ourselves strangled or shot.

Not bad for one night's work, but now we faced another stern challenge: We were hung up in the topmost branches of a very large cottonwood. And in case you didn't know, we dogs are not tree-climbers. We don't climb up trees, and we don't climb down trees either.

And to make matters even worse, we had no idea where we and that tree were located. We might have been in Oklahoma or Kansas or Nebraska, for all I knew, which means that this story might end with us . . .

Gee whiz, just think about the terrible possibilities. We might starve to death in the top of the tree, or fall to our deaths below, or become orphans and vagabonds in a strange location.

And this is Chapter Twelve and we're running out of time and space to come up with a happy ending.

Pretty sad, huh? You bet it was but don't give up yet.

With nothing better to do, we hung onto our respective branches, and I mean hung on for dear life. We got zero sleep and I had to listen to Drover whimper, cry, squeak, and moan for the rest of the night.

Then, at last, I saw the faint glow of morning appear on the eastern horizon. Knowing that the sun could not possibly rise without a good stern barking from the Head of Ranch Security, I was forced to perform this crucial task from the top of the tree.

I mean, if we didn't get that sun barked up, fellers, we might have been stranded in total darkness for days or weeks. So I did my duty and barked it up, and whilst I was in the midst of my Bark Up The Sun Procedure, what do you suppose I heard?

A door slam. Then a voice . . . a voice that sounded slightly familiar . . . a man's voice which said, if I can remember the exact quotation, which said, "Shut up, you idiot dog!"

HUH?

My goodness, that voice sounded quite a bit like Slim's, and then I glanced down and noticed a house down there on the ground, and a tall skinny man, wearing nothing but underpants and boots, standing out on the porch.

Holy smokes, that was Slim the Cowboy! The tornado had carried us two miles down the creek and deposited us in that big cottonwood right in front of Slim's house—what a terrific struck of loke—and all at once I was filled with joy and began barking with all my heart and soul.

Stroke of luck.

And Drover added a few squeaks. His squeaking and my massive barking made just enough noise to draw Slim's soggy red eyes away from ground level and up to the top of the tree.

And at last, yippee, he saw us there! His eyes popped open and his jaw dropped several inches.

And he said—this is an exact quote—he said, "Good honk, I've got huge barkin' squirrels in my tree, where's my gun!"

No, no! We weren't squirrels! It was us, Hank and Drover, his loyal dogs.

Okay, it appeared that he was joking. You know Slim and his warped cowboy sense of humor. It gave me a little scare.

Well, he got a big laugh out of our miserable condition. Yes, while we were up there, clinging for dear life to branches that were rolling like ocean waves in the wind, he got big chuckles.

But suddenly the laughter stopped. He scratched his head and squinted up at us and said, "Hmmm. I wonder how a guy goes about rescuin' two ranch mutts from the top of a cottonwood, 'cause I ain't fixing to climb up there myself. Hmmm."

G.L. Holmes

How did he do it? Well, he called Loper on the phone and Loper came. He had spent most of the night in the cellar, so you can imagine how glad he was to see us dogs up in Slim's tree.

Not glad. Much grumbling and muttering.

But by then he and Slim had figured out how we got there and were ready to call it a good deal. I mean, the tornado hadn't killed anyone or destroyed any ranch property, so they decided to count their blessings.

They got us down, but it was no instant rescue. It took 'em several hours and it ended up involving several of the neighbors, chainsaws, ropes, ladders, and a windmill repair truck with a telescoping crane.

Loper had to pay two hours of rig time on Jay Cox's windmill truck, but I'm sure he considered it a huge bargain. He got his dogs back, that was the important thing.

Well, we had dodged another bullet and had . . . oh, I almost forgot. Sally May never did learn the Awful Truth, that her little stinkpot son had let us into the house that night. But I heard through the grapevine, so to speak, that she found fleas in Alfred's bed.

They weren't mine.

Anyways, it was a great moment in history when Drover and I finally made it back to headquarters and to our gunnysack beds, which is where this had all started, with me and Drover trying to catch a few winks of sleep between assignments.

And that was exactly what I planned to do now. After saving the ranch from the Swirling Killer Tornado, I figured I was entitled to a few winks.

I had just about drifted off into a pleasant dream about Miss Beulah the Collie when I heard Drover's voice.

"Hank, are you awake?"

"Murk snork not if I can help it."

"I was just thinking. Remember that song I wrote about barking at a funnel-shaped cloud? It turned out just that way. We really barked at one. Do you reckon I can see into the future? Gosh, maybe I'm a prophet or something."

I raised my head and managed to open both eyes a crack. "Drover, one of the great challenges we face in this life is trying to distinguish between prophecy and indigestion. Yours was indigestion. Good night."

"It's the middle of the day."

"Shut your trap."

"Good night, Hank."

And with that, we drifted off into our respective dreams and ended another exciting adventure on the ranch.

Case clo . . . snork murk sassafras ZZZZZZZZZZZZZ.